It Sometimes Snows In May
a B.E.A.N. Police novella
By Tope Oluwole

It Sometimes Snows In May
a B.E.A.N. Police novella
By Tope Oluwole

Copyright @ 2009, 2014, 2021 by Tope Oluwole

Published by:

MSCA, LLC

Dedicated to
Oluwadara,
Chinedu,
and Oluwadurotimi,
who remind me daily
that anything can happen,
when you least expect it.

Zota sits hunched over a piece of net-paper, tapping and dragging across its heat-sensitive, plasma interface. Four flexible touch displays engulf him while he backs the darkness, with the exception of a blade of daylight cutting through the brown shutters. In the far corner of the room, the natural light reveals a long dead spider plant.

Computer code fills the displays, while a layout of windowed objects takes up the two center displays. Zota glances at the bottom right corner of the display to his far right. An analog clock pops up, and the computer declares, "eleven-forty-six, A-M." The clock fades away once Zota turns his head back to the code on the screen.

"Not enough time. Not...enough...time," Zota mutters as he types away. "Save and snap," Zota says. An image of a vintage, circular hard disk fades into view on the center-left display.

"Saving..." The computer confirms Zota's command. "Save complete. Creating snapshot... Snapshot complete." An image of a door fades-in on the center-right display, and pulsates with knocking, getting louder. Sweat dots Zota's forehead and neck. The clock fades-in again with the word, "reminder," across its face.

"Crap. She's early," Zota says. He taps through the computer's directory structure, flicking through folders with two sets of his four-in-one cybernetic fingers, until he finds the recently saved file. With a pinch of his sub-fingers across the file, "compressing..." says the computer. The knocking is now loud enough that it drowns out the computer's voice. Once compression of the file is complete, Zota presses on the screen with one of his organic left fingers and drags the file to an image on a mobile device. "Syncing..." the computer replies. Zota clenches his jaw while he reads the progress bar at only three percent, with a duration estimated at twenty seconds. He scrambles in the dark of the room, in his briefs, to find something to put on. "Ow!" Zota stubs his toe on something. A small piece of furniture skids, and something clangs to the ground, then clangs again, before rolling across the floor. Zota tumbles and crashes into something soft. "This better be worth it."

"I was just saying the same thing," a female voice says from beyond the right side of the displays. Zota, still in his underwear, crawls on his hands and knees until he reaches the wall and stands up, facing the light from his now open bedroom door. In the doorway stands a dark and thin figure. The woman steps slowly into the light of the displays, her face weathered with fine lines and a healthy mocha brown complexion baked in. Her boots hit the hardwood floor with a solid clunk as she walks towards Zota. Zota looks over her muscular shape, wrapped in form-fitting jeans in contrast to her green bomber jacket.

"You...you're early Ryles," Zota stutters.

"No, YOU, are late. It's twelve-oh-three already. You need to get your server clock checked. Zota glances back at the right corner of the display closest to him, and the clock pop-up and chimes, "eleven-forty-eight, A-M." The "Sync Complete" message bubble appears over the image of the mobile device. Zota fumbles around his desk, and grabs a thin membrane about half the length of his arm and just as wide. "I don't appreciate having to come and find you," Ryles says. "You really wanna mess with the Triad?"

Zota spies the center of the membrane which also reads, "sync complete", and slaps it across his wrist. It locks and then automatically adjusts to fit, like a band. Zota turns back to Ryles and sees her face is stone; the darkness beneath her eyes, the weariness. "Relax mamita. It's here." Zota taps the band on his wrist. I just wanted to run a final round of Q-A testing to make sure the app can run across different mobile connections. I'm sure your Triad buddies can appreciate that?"

"Save the B-S for your wife. Load it up. I wanna see how it runs."

Zota cracks a smile. "You don't trust me? After all this time?" He extends his arm with the band, and then rolls it behind his back like a magician. Ryles snaps her fingers twice, her scowl deepens. Zota's smile disappears, he brings his wrist forward, facing Ryles. He runs his palm slowly over the top of the band, and the display lights up. He taps the icon of the app, and launches into a series of taps and swipes and finally a shake. All the while Ryles only nods in approval with each action as he completes it.

"Nothing personal, but twenty percent of *nada*, is *nada*. And it's not you I don't trust, it's your habits." Ryles taps her fingers together and then points to Zota's cybernetic four-in-ones. Ryles then motions at the band on Zota's wrist. Zota's presses with two organic fingers on either side of the band. The band releases itself from Zota's wrist with about an inch opening. When Zota touches the band again it straightens itself out completely, while he passes it to Ryles.

"About that twenty percent, change of plan. I'm going with you." Zota waits for Ryles reaction. She smacks the membrane across her wrist which forms the band. "Which means," Zota continues, "I'll be updating your fee down to the escort tier, from the agent tier. In one fluid motion Ryles pulls out an auto-pistol from behind her, and points its silencer-tipped barrel at Zota's head.

"You must be speaking computer code 'cause I didn't hear

that," Ryles replies. "Don't think for a second because you know where all my tattoos are, that I won't split you in two if you try to play me, and collect my twenty percent," Ryles says.

Zota raises his hands, and shows a bright set of porcelain teeth surrounded by a nervous smile. "Hey now... If you're going to kill me...why don't you just take it all?" Zota asks.

"I haven't survived this long in this business by being greedy," Ryles replies. "You might wanna learn something about that." After a few seconds of reading Ryles expression, Zota slowly takes one step forward. Ryles tenses up her right arm, so that it's straight and steady. "Don't be stupid."

Zota stops moving forward. "Then why don't you be smart for the both of us. Just because I'm lousy managing women, doesn't mean I'm lousy with numbers."

Ryles recoils and her eyes narrow. "Huh?" The auto-pistol lowers a couple of inches. Zota lowers himself until he's on his knees, while Ryles follows him with her auto-pistol until the barrel is touching his forehead.

"Just hear me out. The Triad agreed to our two million, with little drama," Zota says.

Ryles shrugs. "It was an offer they couldn't refuse."

"No! The Triad know what this is worth, and they are willing to pay at least ten-times that for the source code and the rights. And...since five percent of twenty million is one million, I believe I just gave you a six-hundred-thousand-dollar bonus. Zota smiles. Ryles eyes soften. Zota turns his head to the side so the auto-pistol runs by his right ear, and Ryles outstretched arm rests on his shoulder.

"What's that old saying?" Ryles asks. "About a bird in my hand is worth two in a bush?"

Zota whispers, "Well you need to get out of the bushes to see the forest for the trees." Zota moves within a foot of Ryles.

Ryles reacts by hooking her shooting arm at a right angle forcing Zota within inches of her face. "But...greedy bastard, we have a contract with the Tri-ad. Do you really want to mess with the Tri-ad?"

Zota replies, "Have the Triad ever...*renegotiated* a contract?"

Elisa peeps through the crack in the office door to see a woman embracing Zota. She turns around, her face pale. Her eyes dart about while she smoothes her hair from her temples back. The ground hums as she tip-toes backwards ten meters to the top of the stairway leading to the office. Elisa then takes a deep breath, exhales, and then forces a smile across her face. "Darling, daaaarling? Where aaaare you?" Elisa sings out loud.

Increasing her place, Elisa eyes glares straight ahead. She bursts through the office door to see Ryles pushing Zota away with force. Zota catches Elisa's eyes, and smirks.

"What's going on here?" Elisa screams.

"Be ready," Ryles says to Zota. She turns away from Zota, and walks out past Elisa without so much as a glance in her direction. Elisa averts her eyes from Ryles as she passes. Elisa watches and waits until Ryles is across the corridor and heading down the stairs, before she turns her full attention back on Zota.

"I didn't think your whoring had become this blatant. I would hope you would at least have a sense of discretion, if not decency. I am a sworn officer of the Commonwealth! I can't afford..."

"Yeah, yeah. You can't afford to manage any scandals you don't know about," Zota says.

"It personally cost me two-hundred thousand dollars to clean up after your last tryst," Elisa says.

"Wow, you got a good deal with today's dollars," Zota replies.

"This isn't a joke Zota! You're jeopardizing my career, my future!" Elisa yells.

"Don't you mean, *our* future?" Zota replies. Elisa slouches and looks down. Her eyes begin to water. "Look. Nothing happened. It's just business. She was getting a bit nervous about our deal, so I needed to calm her down."

"She didn't look very nervous to me," Elisa responds. Zota walks toward a slender Elisa dressed in a cream silk blouse and matching skirt suit. Zota reaches for her ring and bracelet-adorned left hand. Elisa slaps Zota's hands away, one at a time, in a flurry of clumsy but nevertheless accurate swipes. "Spare me the rubbish. I am well aware of your flings with..." Elisa fans her fingers up and behind her towards the corridor.

"Ryles is my agent, baby. I've worked with her for three years and you know this," Zota says holding Elisa at her shoulders.

"Oh, so she's your pimp, and not the other way around?" Elisa asks.

Zota's smile turned to a scowl. "Unlike you, I didn't inherit a trust fund from my daddy, so I've got to hustle, to make sure you can have all the things..." Zota wraps his hands around Elisa's jewelry. "your desk job in the bureaucracy can't afford, while you wait for your payday."

"Don't forget your place!" Elisa snapped. "I married you because you appealed to my father's penchant for seemingly benevolent strays. But make no mistake, you still exist because a *dulcet* willed it!"

Zota fumed in silence as he watched Elisa's red face and flaring nostrils work him over. He swallowed the excess saliva rolling down his throat from having held his breath for so long without realizing it. "What are you doing home so early anyway? Elisa's expression softens. She begins fidgeting with one of her earrings, and then twirls a few loose strands of her blond hair.

"Not like you to have nothing to say," Zota says.

Elisa looks up and lays her hands over her stomach. "Zota...I'm..."

"Oh hell..." Zota begins.

"I'm pregnant," Elisa finishes.

"Are you sure?" Zota asks.

"Bastard!" Elisa blurts at Zota. "Is that your way of asking if it's yours?" Elisa says. Zota shakes his head while pulling up a pair of jeans off the floor. "I'm not the one whoring about!"

"Did you see me..." Zota begins. Elisa puts her palm up against Zota's face. Zota clenches his jaw, and brushes her hand away from his face.

"Spare me the semantics. Whether you like it or not you're the father of my child. I don't want to see that...that...woman, in my house again," Elisa says.

"You don't own me," Zota replies.

Elisa whispers, "Yes I do actually. In case you've forgotten from drowning in so many weekend binges. When we first met, you were a burnt out imitation of cleverness, past your prime, with nothing to show for it but bluster. I admired your passion for life, and in my naivete, your potential. I allowed you a place in my world of resource, power, and import. I can change all that with thirty minutes and a phone. Know your place."

Zota stares dazed at Elisa as she turns around, storms down the corridor, and then down the stairs.

The steel spiral stairs leads into a master living room with a view that could make the cover of a major home design magazine. There are three sofas in view and a motley of oil paintings, bronze statues, and Brazilian cherrywood sculptures. Elisa reaches the bottom of the stairs and then heads across the living room. She sniffs twice in quick succession, gags, and then runs to the kitchen sink; throwing up.

Zota approaches Elisa in a rush from behind. He slinks in behind Elisa, grabbing her by her midsection. Elisa flinches, and slaps behind her, hitting Zota in the face.

Zota staggers back from Elisa stunned. "I meant what I

said." Elisa cleans her face with a sanitary wipe from the dispenser next to the sink. "I don't ever want to see that woman in my house again."

"Come on baby," Zota says. "I just have to finish this deal. Unfortunately, I need *her* to do it."

"You *need* her?" Elisa says. "Or your *penis* needs her?"

"Listen baby. When we first met, I had nothing but loans to collectors, and no clue about what direction I wanted to go in after my father died. I was used to always having someone with the whip to my ass. That someone became you," Zota replies. Elisa sees Zota's face soften. "Now, I feel like somebody worthy of you. Now you don't have to invent some job title when your *plutocrat* friends ask you what your husband does for a living."

Elisa continues to stare at Zota. "So, why her?"

"Why her?" Zota replies, and then shrugs. "I didn't choose her."
Elisa raises an eyebrow. "The client did."

"Does she have to be a *dulcet*?" Elisa asks. "Does she have to be in my house?"

"I don't like it either," Zota says. "But, if I play this right, you can retire early like you're always talking about."

Elisa relaxes her body as Zota pulls her into his embrace. Elisa feigns resistance and then Zota grins. She remains stiff-jawed as their bodies press against each other. Zota grips the back of Elisa's head with one hand, and her right buttock with the other.

"Don't worry," Zota says. "After tonight, you'll never have to see her again."

"Oh, I know," Elisa replies. Zota closes his eyes and presses his lips against Elisa's. Elisa's eyes remain open.

Zota lays flat out on his back snoring. His naked torso and leg pokes out from beneath the bronze, Egyptian cotton bed sheets. Elisa is draped in a pearlescent silk nightie, lying in a fetal position next to him.

Tears well up in her eyes as Elisa pulls the nightie tighter around her breasts. Elisa takes a quick look behind her and watches Zota still asleep, before easing herself out of bed.

Elisa creeps downstairs, through the living room, and finally to the garage. Her hand hovers over a panel which automatically scans her palm. The door slides open to reveal a luxury American truck and Italian sports car.

Elisa's gaze looms on the convertible sports car. Its gleaming red coat beckons her forward. Her gaze shifts to the back wheel.

Twin headlights of a fast moving vehicle speeds down a dark highway. The exhaust note drowns out the emptiness with a clear roar.

A rodent crosses the roadway. Its eyes glow red when the moonlight hits them as it bares metal teeth.

The sports car races past the rodent, barely missing it. Zota changes the music selection with a swipe of his thumb across the touchpad on the right on the steering controls, while Ryles lays in the passenger seat. Zota is clean shaven now, dressed in a white suit, white tie, and black glasses. Ryles, is dressed in leather, and her hair is pulled back into a bun held together by two large pins

"What?" Zota asked.

"I asked you why you have to rub me in your wife's face? She ain't no friend of mine, but it makes it harder to do what we gotta do. I mean, if you can't keep your woman in check..." Ryles says.

Zota smirks. "You want me to get rid of her?" He makes a slice across his neck with his finger tips.

"Seriously Zota," Ryles says. "Hell has no fury as a woman pissed off."

"What? Are you scared?" Zota asked.

"No. But you should be," Ryles says. "She'd get half of everything you own, including your..." Ryles glances sharply at Zota's crotch.

"Look," Zota interrupts. "Like all women, she's got to flex her muscles to feel she's got some sense of control over her man. So, I let her flex. She makes a fuss, then I give her something to take her mind off it."

"What happens when she gets tired of flexin'?" Ryles asks.

Zota looks at Ryles with a confused expression. The sports car roars on. Suddenly the rear tire explodes. Zota yells. Ryles reaches for her pistol. The car shudders, buckles, and then begins to spin out of control to the right side of the road. Zota attempts to steer into the skid, but overcompensates. The car flips violently off the side of the road and down the hill, next to a sign that reads, ISPARI 5 KM.

The car continues tumbling down for about ten seconds before coming to a rest, upside down. The wheels are still spinning, and the once whining powerplant, now lay dead silent, billowing smoke. Glass, liquids, and metal debris strewn the crash site.

A sedan pulls up short of where the sports car tumbled off the road. A shadowed woman is driving. The moonlight reveals a man in the passenger seat, with a thick build dressed in a suit.

Caben shakes his head as he studies the wreckage. "Check? Check what? They've had it. The car must have flipped over twenty-seven times. He makes a repeated looping gesture with his index finger.
Bux replies, "Remember what happened to the last two agents that didn't check if the targets were actually terminated?"

Caben hisses. "Damn! Why do I have to be the one to check?" He rushes out of the sedan, slamming the passenger door behind him.

"Because I rigged the explosive, and I will have the job of making this look like an accident...once you make sure the targets are terminated."

Caben pulls out a pistol with a silencer, and then a flashlight. Following the trail of debris, descends to the crash site.

Bux calls out of the sedan, "Call me on the comm when

you've cleared the site." She grins to herself.

"Okay," Caben replies.

Chunks of aluminum and fiberglass lead Caben down the slope littered with broken branches and upturned dirt. He swats away golf-ball-sized night insects with his flashlight, and uses the barrel of his pistol to push some thorn-laced branches out of his view. Caben hears the hiss of the powerplant get louder as he approaches, before seeing the crumpled car. "Daaaam!" Caben says. His smooth face wrinkles into worry.

"Are the targets dead?" Bux asks over her connection with Caben.

"If they're not, I'm going to start going to church," Caben replies. Caben creeps to the left side of the car, where he sees a bloodied head belonging to a man dangling, but still buckled into the driver's seat. He jabs the body hard a few times with his pistol.

"One down...one to go," Caben says. He tries to see past the driver, but his flashlight fades out. Caben shakes his head. He struggles his way to the other side of the car. It's low enough that Caben takes a handkerchief out of his pocket and lays it on the ground, then places his knee on it, while peering through the branches partially obscuring his view.

The passenger side is empty. Caben scrambles to his feet, and spins around, looking in all directions. Down on the ground he sees shoe prints leading away from the wreck. In the distance Caben hears rustling in the woods to his left. He runs towards the woods.

"What's going on?" Bux says. "You're breathing heavily."

"We've got a live one," Caben replies. "I'm tracking...now." Through the broken path Caben chases through the trees and shrubbery until he passes through a cluster of trees into a clearing. Caben spies a stumbling figure about twenty meters in front of him. Beyond he can hear the rustling of a stream.

"I'm glad I checked," Caben whispers. He then takes a kneeling firing position, shuts an eye, and then fires three shots, his leading arm steady. After the third shot, A scream echoes back towards Caben. The body plunges into the stream.

"Status?" Bux asks.

Caben wipes the sweat off his brow, and then swats at the back of his neck, in response to the buzzing at his right ear. "It's done."

A hover-shuttle races towards the gate on the Ispari side of the demilitarized zone, the sun beaming off its solar cell-lined hull. Black smoke puffs from the left of its twin drives as it burns. A frantic female pilot struggles with the hover-shuttle controls. Next to her is her dead, male co-pilot. Three passengers pull at her chair while screaming at her and each other.

"*M'aider! M'aider!* This is hotel-sierra-one-six-six-tango, requesting emergency support! We are under attack! I repeat, we are under attack!" The pilot screams.

On the ground below a band of five bandits, garbed in a patchwork of ripped beige clothing, fire heavy rifles up at the plummeting hover-shuttle. As the hover-shuttle continues to dive, the bandits mount all-terrain vehicles and pursue it.

"M'aider! New Mass DMZ Tower! We're losing altitude! Request clearance for emergency landing!" The pilot says.

Two bandits race over a dune in their ATVs, followed by a larger vehicle with one driver, and three passengers. Two of the passengers aim surface-to-air weapons skyward. The bottom of the hover-shuttle comes into view, about thirty meters up. Racing and gaining, the larger ATV's passengers fire magnetic grapple lines.

Inside the hover-shuttle, the pilot flinches at the sound of two loud metallic thunks and the cabin floor shudders. "What was that? What was that?" a passenger yells.

"I don't want to die. Today is payday. Don't want to die on pay day," a second passenger says.

"*Merde!*" The pilot blurts out. "Calm down sir! We're NOT going to die!"

"But we're still going to crash!" the first passenger responses.

"We are about to be boarded!" the pilot says. "Everyone assume protective positions!" The pilot engages the autopilot, which then reads, "ENGAGED". The pilot then unbuckles her harness, opens a compartment behind the cockpit, and pulls out a flare gun.

A slim figure with jaggedly cut, wisps of hair limps through an underground bazaar of *daiswright* market sellers, bureau-de-changes, and *excreta* impoverished citizens.

The figure weaves down a tunneled alley of concrete with

dim, green overhead lighting. At the end of the corridor are twin large men of mixed ethnicity, armed with auto-rifles, and an assortment of exotic knives of various shapes and lengths

Before reaching the end of the corridor, the figure slowly raises both her hands and stops before the men.

"They're waiting for me. I am.." Ryles began.

"We will tell you who you are supposed to be, and if you are not, you will never find out if we were wrong," The heavy man on Ryles left says.

His twin on Ryles' right comes across her face with a scanner beam coming from a lens in his left palm. "You look like refuse, but lack the inferiority complex of *excretas*, and most *daiswrights* for that matter. Although, you certainly smell like one," he says. With a flip of his hand back-and-forth, Ryles image compresses into an icon of a lighting bolt on the display on the back of his palm. Seconds later, the heavy receives a sent confirmation on the display.

"You should see the other guy?" Ryles responds.

The second heavy frisks Ryles thoroughly, and pulls out three throwing knives in plain sight. "I figured I'd save you guys the trouble. The palm of the first heavy beeps. He reads the display on the front of his palm, and then a blue light flashes in his earlobe. Ryles forces a grin when they make eye contact.

"Enter, Ryles." The first heavy waves her forward. A thick, metal door slides open and a moving path begins to pull Ryles down a corridor of concrete, lined with scanners. At the end of the corridor, is yet another heavy, identical to the two outside. He waves her politely through another sliding door revealing an elevator.

The third heavy enters behind Ryles and immediately the elevator glides downward. After about a minute, the door on the opposite side from the direction Ryles entered, slides open with hiss.

Ryles recoils as she is greeted by a grated path of flames, ahead of a foyer. "This is new," Ryles says. The third heavy waves Ryles ahead. "You turn down the heat, and I'll be happy to take the lead." The third heavy shoves Ryles out of the elevator. Ryles, sees the flames recede into the grating as she stumbles over the first few grates. When she hears the elevator door hiss closed behind her, she turns around, then looks about her surroundings. "Thanks," Ryles says.

At the clearing ahead is a throne room of concrete. In the center of the room is a robust man in a hover-chair, wearing a peach tunic. He is backing Ryles and addressing three robed figures in stone and metal thrones on net-paper, while the woman directly in front of him concentrates her gaze intensely.

"I like what you've done with the place," Ryles says.

The man on the throne to the left of the woman raises his head from the man in the hover-chair. "Silence!" Third-Thirty booms.

Ryles opens her mouth to speak, but no words come out. Second-Thirty, on the throne to the left, turns his attention to Ryles. Thank you Third-Thirty. After all, a *daiswright* ought to know her place. Director of Protocol (DOP), please receive it at your leisure.

After moments of scribbling, Director of Protocol swivels

around and hovers in front of Ryles. He taps on his net-paper. "Permission to end this session, and begin to receive company, First-Thirty!" Director of Protocol hails.

The woman in the center throne is garbed in a gold embroidered tunic, with matching headdress. She gazes down at Ryles, her eyes a vacant black abyss. Ryles still hasn't gotten used to the sensation of wanting to vomit when making eye contact with any of the Triad. "Permission...granted. Proceed with receiving new company," the First Thirty replies.

The Director of Protocol looks down at the net-paper. "First-Thirty, I..I show no guests on the schedule for today."

"I know. She's tardy by exactly forty-eight hours, twenty-two minutes," Third-Thirty replies. "What is that Ryles?" Ryles attempts to respond, but no sound comes out of her mouth. Third-Thirty rolls his eyes. "Speak!" He flicks his fingers.

"I'm trying!" Ryles blurts out. Oh...better. I know I'm late, but I have what you asked for."

"You will address the excellencies from the circle." Director of Protocol hovers back towards the front of the throne room, while pointing to a raised, metal circle embedded in the concrete where he just left. Ryles limps into the circle about a meter in diameter.

"It seems, Ryles, that you have forgotten your place. Has it really been that long? The contract is clear, the seller must appear at the appointed time. No earlier, and no later. This would classify as later don't you think?" First-Thirty says.

"Yeah, I'm late," Ryles continues. "The seller and I had some trouble on the way here, but I have the ware."

"Unfortunately, per the terms of the contract the seller automatically forfeits twenty percent. I am sure you'll communicate that, in the event there is any dispute."

Ryles lowers her eyes in annoyance, and pulls the band on her wrist off. It's straightened out, and she passes it to Director of Protocol. He in turns inserts it into a slot in his hover chair. A screen materializes downward from the ceiling and icons and text begin to scroll by, first indicating a virus scan, and then an integrity scan. Ryles watches the duration icon fill in and the processing continues. About a two-thirds of the way through, "MEDIA ERROR" appears on the screen. Ryles swears under her breath.

"We are displeased," Thirty-Third says.

"Probably just some dust on the reader," Ryles says. "Just a..a...technical speed bump, I'm sure."

"I will attempt to correct the...technical speed bump, as you call it," Director of Protocol responds.

Director of Protocol clicks and drags on his net-paper, and a, "Repairing..." message pops up on the display. The processing duration icon increases to about 95 percent this time, before it freezes. "MEDIA FAILURE" appears on the display, followed by, "UNABLE TO REPAIR."

"Try it again," Ryles says firmly.

"The media is flawed. The files are inaccessible," Director of Protocol says.

"Do it anyway!" Ryles counters.

Director of Protocol hovers to face Ryles, "It is…"

First-Thirty raises her hand, cutting off Director of Protocol. "It seems you have failed to bring us the ware intact. This too is a violation of the contract, of which the remedies include…death."

"The ware is on there," Ryles snaps. "I saw it myself!"

"That may be factual, but is in dispute if we cannot view the ware, now," Second-Thirty says.

"Perhaps you would like to invoke the half-double-or-nothing clause. It appears to be your only remaining option," Third-Thirty says.

"Excuse me?" Ryles asks with a frown.

Director of Protocol reads from his net-paper, "To preclude
default, the seller or agent representing seller, may request an extension to deliver the ware for a fifty percent discount of the selling price, or dispute the finding of the Triad."

"Fifty percent!" Ryles yells

The Director of Protocol continues, "If the dispute is successful, the Triad will pay double the selling price. If the dispute is unsuccessful, the contract and the seller or agent representing the seller shall be terminated."

"This ain't right. It wasn't…" Ryles begins.

"Do you dare question the integrity of the TRIAD!" The

First-Thirty balls her fist which begins to glow yellow. Ryles becomes engulfed by the same yellow glow, and is then dragged forward while she struggles, towards First-Thirty. She grimaces in pain the most she resists.

"I would recommend you choose quickly, but wisely," Director of Protocol advises.

"Wh...Wh...what are my choices again?" Ryles stutters.

"Request an extension, or request double or nothing," Director of Protocol says.

The Second-Thirty grins. "You are not a *dulcet*, Ryles, so I do not imagine you as a gambler. Although, I would enjoy you attempting to disprove this."

The Third-Thirty smirks. "She may want to ask the seller first. Unless, of course, that isn't an option because we are going to exercise our right in the contract not to allow it."

"Choose!" First-Thirty booms. His eyes glow yellow to orange, then Ryles grabs the sides of her head and screams.

The afternoon sun brings a haze over Ispari gate at the DMZ. Emergency medical personnel race back and forth moving passengers that aren't already dead, from the carnage of a crashed hover-shuttle.

Armored state police-guards hold back the throng of onlookers, including the media, enabling fire department personnel to work on opening the metal grave that is the shuttle, still holding half-a-dozen corpses prisoner.

National guardsmen from New Mass assist in securing the DMZ bridge between Ispari and New Mass, and redirecting traffic.

A tall, lean state police guard, Monavo Morefishco, walks through his subordinate guardsmen at the Ispari gate, and then through the armored riot guardsman closest to the wreckage. He is recognized by everyone he passes with either a nod, or a wave.

"Tell me you caught all the bad guys, nobody died, and I just wasted my time coming here," Morefishco says.

A younger female guard, Practice, nods to Morefishco. "Sorry sir. All the assailants are dead, and so are fourteen of the twenty passengers."

"Oh well. I supposed I should earn my day's pay. What do we got?" Morefishco asks.

"The tower received a distress call this morning about surface-to-air attacks. According to witnesses, the hover-shuttle was shot down, crashed, or both," Practice replied.

"Any of the perps dead?" Morefishco asks.

"We don't have confirmation yet sir," Practice says. "The surveillance video from the tower shows two figures boarding the hover-shuttle, but we haven't identified all the remains yet." She shows Morefishco net-paper with an image of the hover-shuttle. She then presses the play icon over the image.

"Body bandits. It looks like they got in over their heads," Morefishco says.
"Sir?" Practice asks.

"They weren't after the hover-shuttle," Morefishco says. "Any cargo missing?"

"Yes sir. Please, follow me." Practice steps through the debris into the belly of the hover-shuttle amidst the twisted metal, blood, and dust. Morefishco steps through a large tear in the port side of the hover-craft after Practice, and stares at the men, women, and children charred into their protective positions. Morefishco follows Practice, then walks to the rear of the hover-shuttle. She motions for two firemen to open the cargo door. Inside there are just burnt luggage, with the exception of one perfectly intact rectangular, metal box.

"Whatever it was they were after, they were willing to sacrifice a lot for it," Morefishco says.

"I'll ask one of the firemen to open it," Practice says.

Morefishco walks next to the box and notices it is cool to his touch, with blinking lights on one end. "Quickly!"

Practice runs to the front of the wreckage and returns with a squat, balding man in a light armored fire suit. It's coated with the dent, dings, and scrapes of veteran use. They each take places around the box, dragging it out into what used to be the passenger area of the hover-shuttle.

"What is this?" Morefishco asked.

"It's an industrial refrigerator; used to move meat, fish, 'n stuff," the firefighter replies. Morefishco glances at Practice, and then crouches down to attempt to open the fridge, when he sees a biometric access panel below the blinking lights.

Practice looks to the firefighter. "Can you open it?"

"Sure...with a torch." He giggles a bit.

"Get a torch then," Morefishco says.

About fifteen minutes later, the firefighter runs the white hot blast of a laser-torch along the edge of the refrigerator. He's surrounded now by Morefishco, Practice, and the EMTs.

When the firefighter stops the torch, Practice lifts off the dismembered cover, with the help of the EMTs. Inside they see the body of a skinny, middle-aged man, bloodied and bruised. Practice places her fingers along the side of his neck. "I can't feel anything," Practice says.

After tapping some buttons on the device, one muscular EMT places a med-scanner just above where Practice had touched. "I gotta pulse! Very faint!" he says.

"Let's roll," Morefishco replies.

At Zota's residence the following night, a truck stands on the street corner while a torrent of rain beats down on it's metallic black shell. Female fingernails type on a sliver of net-paper furiously. The woman picks up a pair of binoculars from the dashboard. She can see in the magnified view, a luxury sedan parked in front of the garage.
She switches to thermographic view, and her perspective shifts to a glob of red and orange, surrounded by dark blue.

"That didn't take long," Ryles says. She continues typing and an image of a radio antenna appears, along with the message, "Searching for wireless networks..." When "Z-man" appears on the returned list, she selects it with a tap of her finger. "Let's hope I'm luckier than you were Zota."

Ryles taps an icon on the screen with a key on it, and the message, "Attempting to connect..." fades in across the screen. Then, "1st attempt failed." Ryles taps the icon again, and after a few moments receives, "2nd attempt failed." "Retry" and "Cancel" buttons appear on screen as well. "Dang!" Ryles hits the dashboard with the base of her fist.

Ryles drives a rusty truck up the route as the sun peeks over the horizon. She wears a pair of green, convenience-store sunglasses. Her face is bruised, and her lip cut. Her head now wears a buzz cut. After scanning the right side of the road, she slams on the brakes after whizzing by a trail of debris and skid marks. The car screeches to a halt. "Do me a favor Zota and be hanging upside down with a copy of the ware in your pocket," Ryles says.

Ryles climbs down the path to the site of the crash. She finds nothing but twisted carbon fiber and aluminum. A two-hour search of the area reveals no Zota.

Ryles returns to the truck and activates the vehicular computer. She scans the New Mass Gazette for the last two days for any report of the crash. After a few search queries, Ryles finds a short report which reads, "Vehicle accident on New Mass Pike. Occupants missing."

"Dang!" Ryles hisses. From her breast pocket she pulls out her personal digital assistant. She presses the phone icon. "Voice, distort. Dial Zota, home." The device at the other end returns a few long beeps, before a male voice answers. Ryles pauses, before almost stuttering a reply, when she doesn't recognize the voice.

"Ah..Hello. This is Deborah at New Mass Satellite, is this Mister Citysun?" Ryles asks.

"I'm sorry, this isn't a good time. Mister Citysun isn't available." The man responds.

Ryles eyes widen. "Err...Thank you..." Before Ryles can finish her sentence, she hears her PDA alert, "Call ended."

Ryles sips on a mug of liqueur-laced, black coffee at an outdoor table at the Last Breath Cafe in reunified Medford. The heat of the day makes for a damp and muggy night after the earlier downpour. From her table, closest to the trash barrel, and furthest from the rest of the patrons, Ryles stares at the holes in the table.

Suddenly a shadow blocks the light as well as her view of the street. Ryles looks up slowly to see the Director of Protocol and two Triad heavies on each side of his hover-chair. Ryles' face drops to an expression of resignation. She leans back in her chair.

"Have you resolved the problem with the ware?" Director of Protocol hovers so he is looking down at her, even though they both are sitting down.

"I worked it out with," Ryles said.

"Is that right?" Director of Protocol studied Ryles face.

"Yeah. The seller didn't like giving so much up, but he didn't want the alternative either. If you know what I mean?" Ryles said.

Director of Protocol sighs. "I used to believe you were almost as good as your reputation. It looks like you are...to use your street vernacular...slipping. Imagine not knowing your client has met an untimely end."

Ryles can feel her body sweat even more now, but she forces herself to slow her breathing.

Director of Protocol slaps a cut of net-paper onto the table. A glowing ring of red hovers over the lower-left margin, on the list of bookmarks. Ryles reads to herself, the obituary notice for Zota Citysun. She wills back the tears already forming in her eyes.

"I need...a week to filter his place for a copy of the ware." Ryles stares down, her face sullen.

"Are you asking for an extension, Ryles?" Director of Protocol smirks.

Ryles gets up in Director of Protocol's face abruptly. "Look, you piece of..." The heavy on Ryles' right places a larger hand on her shoulder and forces her back down hard on her chair, rattling it and the table beside her. Ryles sits up and slows her breathing again. "I can't stroll into my client's..."

"Former client." Director of Protocol interrupts Ryles

"...house and just start downloading files. I need time. What if it's not in the house? Then I gotta..."

"Do not disappoint me again," Director of Protocol says. "If you disappoint me, you disappoint the Triad."

"Can you buy me a week?" Ryles asked.

"You have 72 hours, per your contract."

Director of Protocol hovers across the street and boards the rear of a taxi van waiting for him and his heavies. The other cafe patrons avert their eyes as they leave. Once they are gone, the couple next to Ryles pass her a few odd glances. Ryles watches until the taxi van drives off, then she slumps back down with her palms over her eye sockets. With her eyes trained on the net-paper, she zooms in on the funeral address.

Outside the entrance to Boylston Cemetery, Ryles watches through the mid-afternoon heat vapors, half-a-dozen people dressed in black. They stand opposite a woman in a off-white robe, reading off a sliver of net-paper. Ryles taps the right stem of her sunglasses, and the view magnifies so that she can now see the face of Elisa crying on the shoulder of a tall, good-looking black man in his fifties.

Beside the man are an older, male *eurasian* couple, and then another mixed sex white couple. Ryles follows them with her gaze as they trail a procession on the path away from the burial site. Ryles looks back at the groundsmen shoveling dirt down in the hole. Ryles taps the mirror function on her sunglasses and examines the cuts on her face which have now scabbed over. After seeing the bags under her eyes, and the fine lines on her forehead, she sighs and taps the stem again. The view returns to the groundsmen.

Ryles steps closer to the edge of the path as Elisa approaches with a tall man by her side in a protective stance. He leaves her no personal space.

Elisa notices an older, rugged-looking woman staring her down from behind her sunglasses.

Ryles intercepts Elisa. "How did Zota die?" Ryles demands. The tall man puts out an arm toward Ryles.

"This is a private ceremony. The Citysun family already delivered a statement at the press conference yesterday. We're sorry if you missed it," Aalin says. He pushes Ryles shoulder back hard enough that Ryles winces in pain. Both Elisa and Aalin stop, and stare wide-eyed.

"Did...Did you know my husband?" Elisa asks, not immediately recognizing Ryles.

Ryles removes her sunglasses. "Yes I did."

Elisa eyes widen and anger fills her face, flushing it red. "You! Have you no shame?" Aalin's jaw tightens, and he reaches for Ryles. Ryles drops her sunglasses on the ground and then grabs Aalin wrist with her left hand until Aalin buckles down on one knee grimacing.

"Your first one was free," Ryles said. "Don't let this one cost you." Ryles applies more pressure on Aalin's wrist forcing his extended arm to hyper-extend further. His eyes shut, and Elisa hears clicks from his arm. Aalin begins to struggle to contain himself. If Ryles didn't have at least a decade on him, she would have no chance to hold him this long. "Now be a nice boy, and pick up my shades so we don't make a scene." Ryles looks up to Elisa. "I know you *plutocrats* don't like to ruffle your feathers." Elisa begins to step back, while Aalin gropes for Ryles sunglasses.

Ryles watches as Aalin reaches them. "Good boy," Ryles said. "Now get up, real slow." Ryles lets go of Aalin's wrist.

Aalin immediately feels cool metal against his neck. "Real slow." He hears Ryles repeat. By the time Aalin is up right he is facing the business end of a pistol.

Ryles catches Elisa easing backwards. "Relax. I'm here to wrap up some unfinished business with Zota."

"Well...as you can see he's dead, so I guess your business will remain unfinished," Elisa says.

"Don't be so quick to throw away money," Ryles replies.

"Excuse me?"

"I'll be coming over for dinner. Seven o'clock. Invite your lawyer too." Ryles puts her sunglasses back on and walks off.

Ryles walks up to the front door of Zota's residence under the cover of another hazy summer night. She tugs down a leather hat matching her jacket, which hides most of her face from the cameras perched around the property monitor.

"Please identify yourself," the residence's artificial intelligence module asks in a voice matching Elisa's.

"Zota's mistress." Ryles smirks.

"Please wait," the residence AI responds.

"Sure."

Moments later, the access panel display next to the door

changes from red, to yellow, to green. "Access granted," the residence AI says. "Welcome." Ryles hears the doorbell chime inside, and a few seconds later. The front door slides open to reveal Elisa. She stares down Ryles; her face scrunches up as if she's tolerating a foul odor.

"How quaint," Elisa says. Elisa leads Ryles in. Ryles watches Elisa glide through the living room which has been upgraded with larger, plush furnishings worthy of an old English castle. At the grand, wood-trimmed table, Elisa sits at the head with Aalin to her immediate right, and a pigtailed, *blasian* man in his sixties on her left.

"So...to what do I owe this visit, from someone I never expected to see...in my house...ever again?" Elisa says. She passes Aalin a side glance.

"The brother with the sore wrist I know." Ryles points to Aalin. "So I hope the skinny, old guy is your lawyer."

"The best ones are," Elisa replies.

"Zota and I have a business agreement..."

"Oh! Is that what you *daiswrights* are calling adultery now?" Elisa interrupts.

Ryles picks up one of the marble coasters on the table, feels its weight in her palm, and then slams it on the table. Everyone flinches, and Elisa gasps, eyeing the table where the coaster lay. "Pay attention, or you'll miss the good part. I found a buyer for some ware your husband wrote. The copy he gave me to deliver doesn't work. I need another copy so I can close the deal."

Elisa let out a dramatic laugh. "That's preposterous!"

"That's why your lawyer's here," Ryles says.

Ryles pulls out of her coat, a rolled up piece of net-paper, and passes it to Elisa's lawyer. Elisa and Aalin look at each other. Both their smiles are gone.

Elisa's lawyer begins to read, and then taps the net-paper and swipes upwards, scrolling through the text. He stops, then compares Zota's signature on another net-paper document, with that of the document Ryles provides. He scans over both documents with the face of his left palm. A light-blue beam washes over both documents. After about five minutes, a low chime emits from the lawyer's hand. A green light flickers on and stays steady.

"Well Wellington?" Elisa asks the lawyer.

"The biometric signatures on this contract between Miss Ryles, and Mister Citysun are authentic.

Wellington approaches Elisa with both net-paper documents, but Aalin intercepts it. After Aalin reads the documents, he turns to Elisa, nods, and then hands them over to her. Elisa flicks at the net-paper, whizzing through the contract. She stops at the dollar amounts, and then to the biometric signatures. She studies Ryles' image, a younger version, and bristles.

"So, how much am I receiving, as Zota's legal beneficiary?" Elisa asks. Wellington nods in agreement.

"Well my cut's twenty percent, leaving Zota one-point-six million," Ryles said.

Aalin Flashes Elisa a look. "Really?" Elisa meets his eyes, and then she focuses back on Ryles. "Well, how does this all transpire?"

"Same as always. I close the deal, get my cut, forward the rest to the seller," Ryles says.

Elisa and Aalin laugh. "We may be *plutocrats*, but we're not above worrying about money. How can we be sure you won't take the prize and run?" Aalin asks.

"You guys are obviously new to this," Ryles says. "Zota was green, but even he knew better than to…"

Before Ryles can react, Aalin pulls an auto-pistol on her, and two red dots dance around her forehead like fireflies.

"Whoa." Ryles smirks. "You damn government net-paper pushers are trying to hustle me? Do you know who the buyer is?"

"For that kind of money there's only one place," Ryles says. Aalin and Elisa look at each other. "That's right."

"You think you two can just stroll into the bazaar?" Ryles asks. "I know people with new money can do some stupid things, but don't make this one of them?"

"Oh no. You're going to take care of the formalities," Elisa says. Elisa turns to see the look of apprehension on Wellington's face.

"Thank you for your time," Aalin waves Wellington away with his un-bandaged hand. Wellington hesitates and meets Elisa's eyes.

"It's all right, I'll ring you tomorrow," Elisa says.

Wellington clutches his briefcase, and then rises. He nods approvingly at Ryles, and then walks around the table toward the front door. When Wellington passes Ryles, she grabs him tightly against her bosom, and then presses the nose of her drawn pistol to his temple. Aalin holds out his un-bandaged hand toward Ryles with even calm across his face.

Wondering how I got past your security with this, huh? Well, I'd ask whoever did your security," Ryles says to Elisa.
Elisa glares at Aalin. Ryles grins and then eyes Aalin, Elisa, and the two shadows on the second-story landing picked up by her sunglasses' heads-up-display.

"Please leave Wellington out of this. He has a wife and child to go home to," Elisa says.

"How big of you. Here I am just trying not to get shot at by the two jokers on the second floor. How selfish of me," Ryles says. Elisa grits her teeth.

The front door slides open once Ryles steps on the pad in front of it. She steps backwards through the door with Wellington, and disappears.

Three months later, at East Ispari Hospital, a nurse walks through an intensive care ward with a food cart. As she passes two other nurses, one male nurse teases her. "Time for your dinner date already, Lisa?"

"Be nice Laban," Lisa says.

"Yeah, yeah. I know...The dead can still hear you. At least

you know why he never calls," Laban says.

Both nurses crack up laughing as Lisa enters a room two doors from the nurses' station. As she's done for the last three months, she immediately goes to the curtains and draws them closed.

"Hello John." Lisa smiles at the withered black man laying in the bed. "You missed the fireworks last night. They were beautiful."

She checks the monitors adjoining his bed for heart rate, blood pressure, and other vitals. They are below normal, but steady, as always. Lisa looks over the man older than his stats indicates, his cuts and bruises healed, but with scars remaining. "Well, tonight, we are going to watch *Independence Day*. It's a classic. I know we normally watch Ispari Vice on Fridays, but I'm feeling patriotic." Lisa giggles. The man remains motionless, eyes shut, an array of nodes, tubes, and nanotechnology keeping him alive. "I think you'll like it. You look like a fighter, and this movie is about fighting."

An hour later Lisa locks her gaze to the display watching antique *fighter jets,* as they used to be called, take out enemy spaceships, when her PDA chimes. Lisa looks at the caller id, exhales, and takes the call as she walks out of the room.

Moments later the heart rate display ripples to life with beeps and violently jagged topography. Soon the man's closed eyelids begin to pulse. When Lisa returns to the room, she drops her PDA and stumbles backwards a step once she sees the man on the bed.

The next morning Morefishco trails Lisa into the man's hospital room. The man is sitting upright in the center of the bed wearing a patient smock. He looks up to his visitors with apprehension.

"Good morning John." Lisa forces a smile. "This is Ispari State Guard Morefishco.

Zota looks to Morefishco in resignation. "She wasn't kidding when she said I'd been in a coma, in Ispari, for the last three months?"

"I'm afraid so." Morefishco studied the man's face.

"How did I get here?" Zota asks.

"What's the last thing you remember, before you woke up?"

"A red sports car." Zota narrows his eyes. "I was driving…"

"What else?" Morefishco can see the man straining. "Take your time."

"There was an explosion…" He places a hand on his temple. "Spinning. Everything started spinning."

"He needs to rest." Lisa says to Morefishco, but is still staring at the man. Lisa walks towards him and then lays him back down on the bed.

"That's all I remember," he says.

Morefishco moves to the bed beside the man. "Can you give me just a couple more minutes with him?"

Lisa is about to protest when she gets a ping on her PDA,

and frowns. "Make sure it's just a couple of minutes. I'll be right back." Lisa smiles at the man, who returns a weak smile and a half wave.

"It's okay. It looks like I'm in good hands," The man says.

The man spies the auto-pistol in Morefishco's holster. Morefishco waits until Lisa leaves and the door slides and hisses shut behind her.

"She keeps calling me John because neither of us know who the hell I am. She called you when the hospital couldn't find anything, since my identity chip is missing," he says.

"Your chip was gone when we found you. Nice and clean cut too. You had no other ID on you. The strangest thing is, no one has reported you missing, or come looking for you since."

The man runs his finger over a hairline scar on his forearm. "Since? Since what?"

"Three months ago, *excreta* body bandits attacked a hover-shuttle by the DMZ." Morefischo studies the man's facial response.

"What does that have to do with me?" The man asks. His face twists in confusion.

"We found you on ice in a body box," Morefishco says.

"A what?"

"A refrigeration unit for transporting large amounts of organs." Morefishco smiled at the man. "You're one lucky son of a gun." The man looked up with fierce eyes. "I know it doesn't look that way from where you're sitting. But trust me on this one. I was there."

Running his hand through his hair and then feeling his naps with the palms of his hands, the man gasps.

"I'm sure this is a lot to take in, but we need to know who you are, and why you were smuggled in a hover-shuttle," Morefishco says.

"I..I don't know. Still trying to wrap my head around this whole thing." he stops, then scratches his head. "I don't remember anything before the drive. Or after." The man drops his head between his hands.

Morefishco waves until he gets Lisa's attention, as she stares at the man from outside the room. Morefishco turns back to the man. "Well, someone wanted you badly enough. Body bandits willing and able to take that kind of risk aren't cheap. That means someone's gonna come looking for you sooner or later." Morefishco turns to Lisa. "This room is gonna be on lockdown until further notice."

"Lock down?" Lisa asks.

"There'll be a guard outside his room at all times. No one besides you and his primary doctor comes in here without my say so," Morefishco says.

"I don't think we have to go that far. Your alarming John," Lisa says.

"John?" Morefishco's looks at Lisa, and then at the man, who shrugs in resignation. "Sure."

"Besides, no one knows he's here but us," Lisa says.

"I'm about to change that," Morefishco says.

Several nights later Ryles sits against the headboard of a hotel room bed. She wears her hair short and curly, from a styling kit she picked up at a convenience store a block away from the hotel. Her Big, gold, door-knocker earrings, swing and shine in the lowlight of the room. A blue light glows on the end of each earring. The in-room display suspended above the foot of the bed blares out world news. The red sundress she's in shows the scars on her legs barely noticeable under her expensive, but hurriedly applied, makeup. Ryles nods and continues her seemingly one-sided conversation.

"I'm sure they haven't forgotten about me. This ware is something they want more than money. I had to disappear when things went south with the client."

Ryles nods a couple of times before continuing. "If you're sure they're going for the termination clause, then I guess I'd better come up with a plan B."

Ryles disconnects her call with a swipe of her right earring. She looks up to the live news report. "Increase media volume twenty percent," Ryles commands.

"Male, black, mid-thirties...Ispari State Guard would like anyone with any information on a John Doe, in his mid thirties, to contact them at @TIPO-ISG or tips@ISG.gov"

Ryles strains to study the man on the display with bushy hair and a full mustache and beard. It takes her about ten seconds before she recognizes him. "Zota." She scrambles to her feet and scurries up to the display until she's half a meter in front of it. "I can't believe it. You son-of-a-bitch. You're alive! My payday is alive, and I better get my ass in gear to claim it, before someone else beats me to it."

Ryles swipes her right earring again, and initiates an outgoing call. She's pacing back and forth on the memory mattress, pulling down her dress and smoothing it out. The call connects.

"Ispari State Guard. Can I help you?" a woman asks.

"Thank you Jee-sus," Ryles says.

"Ma'am?"

"You found him! You've found my brother," Ryles says. "I just saw the news broadcast about the Joe Doe."

"You'll need to come down to our headquarters, and ask for Guard Morefishco. Let me give you the address…"

The next morning, a black man, in his sixties knocks at a motel room door. Ryles answers it wearing a denim skirt, a snug and revealing blouse, and three-inch, open-toe high heels. Her face is made up heavy to enhance what nature and life had laid on her. She even managed a manicure and pedicure.

Ryles lets in a man wearing a work overalls with *James* embroidered over one of the breast pockets, and a toolbox in his left hand.

"What took you so long?" Ryles asks. "The *guardies* are gonna be expecting me this morning. You get everything?"

James plops his toolbox on the desk across from the bed. He opens it up, and pulls out net-paper of various sizes, ID cards, flash chips. "Hey queenie, you just can't pick these up at your local office supply store." He pulls up an ID card with thumb and retinal biometric output panes. "New state ID for Maria Brown, ground vehicle license, passport. I also set up financial records, relational history, back ten years…including your wedding to Mister Brown. And, since you're one of my favorite, if not best looking, customer's, I threw in wedding images, and courtship e-mails…"

"Damn." Ryles blushed. "How well will it hold up?"

"It'll be fine…as long as they don't dig deeper than Misses and Mister Brown. The fake friends are hologram thin, so if some *guardie* with a hard-on goes hunting for your maid-of-honor, you may have some explaining to do. Unless you want to go for broke and get some cyber-actors?"

"Huh?"

"It's the latest thing in the bazaar. Unemployed and aspiring actors are getting cybernetics to play any a-list actor they can dream of. It's their edge to break into the biz. They can be anybody you want them to be." James smiles.

"How much is that gonna set me back?"

"If you have to ask…" James lays a net-paper on the table facing Ryles.

Ryles glances at the price matrix. Her eyes widen. "I'll take my chances."

"I figured as much," James says.

"How much do I owe you?" Ryles asks.

"three-fifty," James says. "And before you have a little heart attack, that includes the first and last month's rent for the furnished house."

Ryles sighs. "Where?"

"I know what you're thinking. It ain't no mansion. But, it's a nice and respectable, everyone-minds-their-own-damn-business neighborhood in New Neasden."

"Okay." Ryles pulls out a department store shopping bag from under the bed, and holds it against her. "There's three in here…"

James frowns.

"I wasn't expecting that much, and it's all I can get right now, without raising alarms." Ryles stares at James and watches him size her up. "It's in cash James, and you know that ain't easy."

"I'm impressed."

"You'll even be more impressed, when you count it." Ryles closes the space between herself and James to about a meter.

"Hey, I'm old school," James says. "You know I'm gonna count it." He continues to study Ryles. James grabs the bag from Ryles and immediately feels the weight. He pulls it up and peeks inside. "I hope he's worth it." James smiles.

Ryles squeezes James' shoulder as he leaves, then closes the door behind him. "Thanks dad."

Ryles pulls down the street in a hover-car, from a tall glass and metal, cone-shaped building. She glances at her PDA as the vehicle auto-parks. The time on the marquee display belonging to the bank across the street, reads 12:07 PM. Ryles heads towards the gleaming tower with, ISPARI STATE GUARD HEADQUARTERS, in neon, scrolling across the main entrance.

As she climbs the front stairs, miscellaneous uniformed and non-uniformed personnel and citizens march out and stroll in by her. Some pass her a casual glance as she fans her chest in the noonday heat.

Once Ryles passes the sliding door she's scanned by an electronic eye above the main sliding doors, and is then greeted by a virtual female desk *guardie*.

"Welcome to Ispari State Guard Headquarters, Misses Brown. How may I be of service today?" The virtual *guardie* asks.

"I'm here to see...Morefishco, about my missing brother," Ryles says. She looks at her PDA to double-check the name.

"One moment please." The virtual *guardie* blinks her eyes in time with the data processing she's performing. After a few moments, a copy of the virtual *guardie* appears beside Ryles. "Follow me, please."

Ryles tries not to look alarmed and follows the virtual *guardie* copy to the smart lift. They are carried silently up several floors. When the smart lift doors slide open, a lean but muscular, caucasian man in his late fifties in uniform awaits them.

"Guard Morefishco. This way Misses Maria Brown," the virtual *guardie* says.

"Thanks Vidge." Morefishco watches the virtual *guardie* dematerialize. "Afternoon, Misses Brown. Thank you for coming. This way please." Morefishco begins down the hall, but waits for Ryles to catch up before getting too far ahead.

"When can I see my brother?"

Morefishco casts Ryles a look. "We just have to take care of some minor bureaucratic details."

"Like what?"

"I'm sure this is a lot to take in, but we have to go through a quick ID verification process. Just a formality. I can't tell you how many times some missing guy turns up, and half the women in Ispari show up claiming to be a wife, girlfriend, or grandmother." They both walk past an office with ISG. M. Morefishco glowing within the glass of the door.

"Yeah..It is a lot," Ryles says.

Morefishco leads Ryles into a room with camoglass. Ryles can feel her neck turn warm. "Why are we here? Where is my brother?" Ryles asks.

"Please sit down Misses Brown." Morefishco gestures towards the chair opposite him and then waits until Ryles sits down, before doing the same. "For security, I need to verify some information. The man we have in custody doesn't know his own name." Morefishco pauses and stares at Ryles, who in turn leans forward in her chair.

"What? He doesn't know who I am?" Ryles points a finger towards her chest. "When he sees my face..."

"Can I see some identification, Misses Brown. A quick scan should speed this up for both of us," Morefishco says.

Ryles pulls her Maria Brown license out of her bag, and places it on the table in front of Morefishco, showing off her manicure. A neon blue square appears within the table and shrinks, until it perfectly fits the perimeter of the license. Morefishco slides the net-paper, card stock off the table, and studies it for several moments, occasionally glancing back at her.

Suddenly, a display rises out of the table, visible only to Morefishco. It begins scrolling information of Mary Brown of Ispari. The record includes a residence address, vehicle registration, and some traffic violations. Towards the end, the record shows social networking records. "What's your brother's name?"

"Roberto." Ryles stares at Morefishco who is still scanning the record.

Morefishco taps on a relationship link leading to Roberto Brown; the third Brown on the list. The image renders. It resembles a clean-cut version of the John Doe Morefishco has in custody.

"You'll be happy to hear you're not one of the usual characters we get." Morefishco taps the top edge of the display firmly. The display powers itself off, and then slowly slides back into its place embedded in the table

"Nice to know," Ryles says.

Morefishco studies Ryles for a moment. "I'm curious Misses Brown, where did you file a missing persons report for your brother? I didn't find any record of one being filed in the state."

"My brother kinda does his own thing. It's not unlike him to fly off to Brazil for a month and not tell anybody. I didn't know he was missing until I saw him on TV."

"I see." Morefishco gave Ryles an even expression. "I guess you guys aren't close then?" Ryles responded with a scowl. "Sorry, occupational hazard. I can't help but ask."

"No, we don't swap recipes or bitch about our exes," Ryles says.

"What about his family?" Morefishco leaned in, resting his forearms on the table.

"Family?"

Morefishco recoiled. "You know...Wife, ex-wife, kids, a dog, a cat, a snake... People who might give a crap if he was missing for three months."

Ryles lowered her head, and hunched over, which inadvertently made her look softer to Morefishco; less *I-don't-need-no-man*, and more *I-got-problems-but-doesn't-everyone*. I'm the only *family* he's got left.

A light on the top of the display in the table glows green. Morefishco pushes down on the top of the display which toggles it back up to face him. "Can I speak with you sir? It's important", appears in an alert message on the screen. Morefishco stares at the message for a moment, then closes the display.

"Are we done?" Ryles asks.

"Almost. I'll be right back." Morefishco exits the interrogation room from a different door than they had entered, and walks into a back room where a junior *guardie* and John are waiting.

A bony young man rises at Morefishco's entrance into the room. "He said he recognized her."

Morefishco turns to John. "This is your sister?"

"Well, I remember her face..."

"Is she your sister, or isn't she?" Morefishco's face turns pink.

"I remember her face" John nods "And her voice."

Morefishco scowls at the junior *guardie*. "You interrupted my interrogation for this? I remember the voice of President Obama; doesn't make him my cousin."

"It's what I remember," John says. He walks to the one-way camoglass separating and obscuring the inner room from the outer room where he stands. The glass is cool to his touch as he presses his palms against it, and stares at the mocha-skinned woman.

"Patel, you know how many weirdos we've had in here since the broadcast? I almost regret authorizing it," Morefishco says.

"I know this, but she is the only one he *recognized,*" Guard Patel says.

"I'll bet," Morefishco hisses.

"You can't prove she's not my sister." John turns to Morefishco. Guard Patel swallows. Morefishco can't see his tan face go crimson.

"And you can't prove she's not one of the bandits that put you on ice!" Morefishco stands in front of John. "Did you ever think of that?" The room is silent.

"If it makes you feel better, you can keep an eye on me. I mean her. Well, us…" John says.

"And waste more taxpayers' bitcash? I don't think so." Morefishco steps out in front of John and extends his hand to the door separating them from Ryles. "Go say hi to your sister." Patel's eyes widen, but Morefishco doesn't react to it. He opens the inner door, and lets John through.

Morefishco and Patel watch as John walks in and begins to observe Brown. The inner door slides shut, separating them.

Ryles watches a thinner but healthier Zota walk towards her. He cracks a half-smile and shuffles his feet. At about a foot from the table, he puts out a hand on the chair opposite Ryles. Immediately Ryles rises from her seat and runs around the table, reaching for Zota. She places her hands on each side of his face and then hesitates before slipping them around his neck. Her eyes water as she pulls him into a fierce hug.

From the inner room Morefishco and Patel watch the

embrace, and then at each other. "That don't mean frack, Patel. Get a cyberdog and track them." Before Patel could protest, Morefishco waved him down. "Got a warrant, and had him chipped and coded while he was still under. I'm not taking any chances."

"You do not believe Misses Brown is his sister?" Patel asked.

"Your sister ever hug you like that?" Morefishco asked. Patel shook his head. "She's no body bandit, but by the look of her, she's been around the block more than a few times, and I'm sure she knows how to handle trouble."

"Really? What if the people, those...body bandits come after him?" Patel asked.

"That's what I'm counting on?"

Zota and Ryles walk out of the headquarters building. The sun low in the sky makes Ryles shield her eyes, until her sunglasses can auto-adjust. She moves briskly, slightly ahead of Zota.

"Are you sure you're not my sister?"

"Damn. The *guardie* wasn't kidding when he said you lost your memory." Ryles glances behind her as they cross the street towards her ground vehicle.

Three figures dressed like *excretas,* after a long day at the plant, join two others on the side of the street Ryles crossed to.

"I thought you were dead Zota. I didn't know different until the *guardies* did a broadcast about a John Doe from the hover-shuttle crash at the DMZ," Ryles says.

"I remembered your face. You were driving a car. I was in the car with you… Then an explosion. The car was spinning," Zota says. Ryles nodded. "I don't remember anything before or after that. Morefishco told me he found me in a body bandit fridge, or something."

"Body bandits? Damn. No wonder Morefishco wasn't too crazy to see me. How many people did you see before I showed up?"

The *excretas* close in on Ryles and Zota.

"About two dozen." Zota grinned.

Ryles unlocks her ground vehicle with a swipe of her hand against a reader embedded in the door panel. Once they are both in the vehicle, Ryles eases the vehicle into the street. "Cloud plate." Ryles commands. The vehicle registration external placard image becomes obscure for a few seconds before its characters morph into a different registration alphanumeric. A block, and two turns later, Ryles glances in the rear view display, and notices the same car has been pursuing them since they got into the vehicle.

"What?" Zota asks.

"That black van has been following us since we left *guardie* HQ." Ryles says, cutting her eyes to the rear view display.

The van slips in and out of traffic until it catches up with Ryles' vehicle. Ryles takes a sharp swerve into a narrow side street, scaring few citizens senseless.

"You think they're after us?" Zota asks

"I know they're after you. I just happen to be tagging along." Ryles says.

Ryles' vehicle makes another sharp turn into what appears to be a dead-end road, but leads into an industrial park. Zota looks into the passenger's side rear display, and sees a figure lean out of the window of the van, with a shoulder-mounted something.

"Now would be a good time to lose the guys behind us. I'm not in
any hurrying to be in another ice box.

Ryles looks in the rearview display embedded in the dashboard. "They wouldn't blow up this ride." Zota turned to her. "They can sell it once they get rid of us." Zota's eyes widen. "They just want us to pull over."

"Pull over?" Zota asks, deadpan. Ryles doesn't answer, just grins.

The bandit leaning out of the van window fires a round out of his shoulder-mounted launcher. The large capsule-like projectile whistles through the air toward Ryles vehicle.

Alarms blare from the Ryles' vehicle speakers. INCOMING MISSILE flashes across the screen of the vehicular computer. On its display, a red dot moves closer and closer to a green dot moving in the same direction, but much slower in comparison.

Ryles swerves the vehicle hard left and drives towards an alley between two warehouse buildings. "Hang on!"

The capsule breaks on impact against the rear deck of the vehicle. A gelatinous mass sticks to the hull, and begins to grow a red spike. The spike digs into the metal of the hull, burrowing inside.

"No boom?" Zota asks.

The dashboard lights begin to flicker, and the vehicle begins to lurch forward. "EMP...I'm losing power," Ryles yells.

As Ryles' vehicle slows to a crawl, the bandits speed closer. "Get ready to bounce out the car quick," Ryles says. Zota nods. "Get my gun." Ryles taps a button on the navigation controls, which opens a compartment above Zota knees. Zota tentatively pulls the auto-pistol out of the compartment.

Their vehicle crashes into the corner of one of the buildings. Ryles and Zota scramble out of the vehicle and down the alley, as smoke fills the air around them. "Hold your breath, and move!" Ryles pushes Zota ahead of her. After about five seconds of break-neck speed, Ryles spins around, and begins firing down the alley in the direction they came from. The bandits back-up momentarily, taking cover behind Ryles' vehicle. Ryles taps her smart-watch twice. "Come on."

Ryles and Zota duck down a cross street. A loud explosion in the distance startles Zota, but he keeps running.

Elisa and Aalin stand in the upstairs hallway of Elisa's mansion. Elisa is dressed in a pearlescent skirt suit, while Aalin dries his face with a towel. The monogram on the bathrobe he's wearing read, "ZC".

"You said he had been taken care of," Elisa says.

"What's this all about." Aalin slips both arms around Elisa, resting his large palms on her buttocks. "Bad day at the office?"

"Don't try to butter me Aalin, it's ill-advised. I'm hardly in the mood." Elisa lightly smacks Aalin's arms down, and slips out of his grasp.

Aalin's smile disappears. "Okay… What happened?"

"This." Elisa puts her PDA in Aalin's face and taps a button to stream a video. It's a newscast featuring Zota as John Doe. Aalin's face hardens as he watches the highlights of the video.

"Where did you get this? How do you know it isn't some hoax," Aalin says.

"Because the individual who sent this to me, knew he was my husband," Elisa says.

"Do you recognize the address?" Aalin asks.

"No. It came in as spam," Elisa says.

"Did you reply?"

"Reply?" Elisa walks to the railing. "I deleted the blood e-mail."

"Don't worry, I'll take care of it personally," Aalin says.

"No! No more skullduggery," Elisa says.

Alan recoils. "Are you getting sentimental?" Aalin watches Elisa's face intently. "I have no interest in going to prison."

"Don't get nervous. It doesn't suit you." Elisa get up close to Aalin. "All this person knows is that Zota was my husband. Zota clearly can't confirm that or he wouldn't be a John Doe, and the Ispari authorities would have contacted me by now.

"So what's the plan?" Aalin leans against the railing looking at Elisa. Elisa in turn begins rubbing her hand across his bare chest.

"Keep it simple silly. I will go to Ispari and get my ex-husband. Then you will see to it that he has a more permanent retirement," Elisa says.

Ryles opens the door with her fingerprint and voice activation through an access panel in the front door. The door slides open. Ryles stumbles in, and then collapses on a plush, beige couch.

Zota enters the room after Ryles, and examines the apartment with an open floor plan. A kitchen to the left with an adjoining bar to the right of the door, while the living-room where he finds Ryles sprawled on the coach. On the corner table Zota sees an oil painting of the two of them, with Ryles leaning against him.

"Soooo...what's going on?" Zota asks.

"The bad guys didn't get you today," Ryles replies. "You can thank me later."

"Who are you? And don't tell me you're my sister," Zota says.

Ryles takes her hands off her face and look up to the ceiling. She presses a couple of buttons on her PDA. Moments later a house robot, about the size and shape of a ottoman, brings her a glass half-full of whisky. Its aroma invades Zota's senses and brings about a frown of recollection. "Didn't we already go through this?"

"You had me going until I saw that picture. I had a flashback of you kissing me." Zota circled around the couch while running his finger along its spine, until he goes behind Ryles. Then Zota knelt so his head was now behind hers. "It felt like someone lit a match and kept it just far enough away from my mouth not to burn."

Ryles could feel his hot breath at the back of her ear, and then down her neck. "Don't get it twisted. You don't know me like that…" Zota lays his hand on Ryles shoulder, and lets it rest there. His head now besides hers. Ryles head resting and still tilted up, focused at no point on the ceiling in particular.

"Then there was the way you handled Morefishco, and those bandits in the alley. You didn't even blink. I just about pissed my pants," Zota says. "You're *daiswright*, ex-militia or something, right?"

"I…I'm a teacher," Ryles says.

"What martial arts?" Zota says. "Then teach me."

Zota closes in on Ryles until his lips are inches from hers. Suddenly, Ryles whips out an auto-pistol and jams it against Zota temple. Zota winces. His mind flashes back to being back in a sports car, driving down a deserted road with Ryles in the passenger's seat. Ryles mouths something. "I *said*…we don't have that kind of relationship."

Zota opens his eyes, the metal of the barrel presses deep into his temple.

"Easy, easy. I'm gonna get up, go into the bathroom, and take a cold shower now. Right after I change my drawers," Zota says.

"You're not going anywhere." Ryles rotates herself off the couch with the auto-pistol still pointed at Zota. Zota can feel his knees begin to throb as he remains behind the couch.

"Are you a bounty hunter?" Zota asks. "Whatever they're paying you, I'm sure we can work something out."

"It's kinda nice to see you on your knees. I think I like the new *you* better," Ryles says. "Plus, I'm not interested in turning you in for cash. I don't hate you that much. You and I…"

"Dating? Yeah, I guessed that much. So what went wrong? You caught me with another woman? I'm sure it won't do any good to say, 'I'm sorry, but I don't remember," Zota says.

"Ha ha!" Ryles steps back a bit. "I *like* the new you, but please don't ruin it by getting off your knees." Ryles circles around the couch and behind Zota, and then quietly slips her auto-pistol back into her thigh holster. Oh we were in a relationship…a business relationship. What went wrong was that the ware we were supposed to deliver doesn't work, so we didn't get paid.

"Is there a back-up?" Zota asks.

"Oh yeah," Ryles says.

"How do you know?"

"I know you," Ryles says. "And for both our sakes, there better be."

At Ispari State Guard Headquarters, Morefishco sits at his desk running Zota's picture against images in a federal database. Moments later Patel appears at Morefishco's open door, and knocks.

"Can I speak with you?" Patel asks.

Morefishco waves in him quickly with irritation and brings his attention back to his desktop display. Images are still flying by on the screen. Patel steps in and then stands in front of Morefishco cluttered desk.

"The John Doe person you asked me to track…"

Morefishco looks up. "Don't tell me, his sister killed him?"

"Um no…but if she is a teacher, then I am a boy scout," Patel says.

Morefishco rolls back in his seat and lets out a laugh. "But you *are* a boy scout."

Patel grins and passes Morefishco a slip of net-paper. "Surveillance cameras caught Mary Brown in an altercation with a group of body bandits. John Doe was with her."

Morefishco taps on the net-paper and watches play-back of the body bandits chasing Ryles and Zota, and ends with an explosion. "I see Brown shooting, and I see the explosion, but I don't see any bodies."

"Nothing could have survived that," Patel says.

"Don't be so sure."

"She's not a school teacher chief," Patel says.

"I know, but if Brown wanted John Doe dead, he would be already. There's something else going on and we need Mary Brown to lead us to it." Morefishco's PDA chimes. He picks it up on the second chime.
"Morefishco? They want what? Tell that wacko that kidnapping is still against the law and we can trace his call if he doesn't politely hang up."

Patel looks to Morefishco. His eyes wide. He watches Morefishco listen for a few seconds, all the while trying to get a word in edgewise.

"I can't release him, because he's already gone...excuse me? His wife? New Mass Congresswoman Citysun?" Morefishco's eyes squeeze shut. "Hold on." Morefishco taps mute on this PDA and swivels to Patel. "Grab Practice, and pick 'em up. Right now!"

"Pick up who, chief?" Patel asks.

"Hansel and Gretel. Who do you think?"

Patel scurries out of Morefishco's office. Morefishco waits until Patel closes his door, and then returns his attention back to his PDA. "Put Congresswoman Citysun through."

Ryles strolls into the living room of her apartment house

wearing jeans and a tank-top. Her hair is wrapped in a white towel, and her feet bare. Ryles stares at Zota laying on the couch with a slip of net-paper in his hands. On hearing Ryles enter he straightens up.

"Good morning sunshine. I made some breakfast. It's in the microwave. I didn't realize you were going to sleep-in this long," Zota says.

"You made breakfast?"

"Yeah." Zota pauses. "Is that allowed?"

Ryles nods and cracks a tiny smile. "Thank you."

"You should smile more often," Zota says. "You seem like you'd be fun to be around. When you're not killing bad guys of course."

Ryles' frown returns as she walks into the kitchen.

"So who are you, really? You're sure not looking to kill me, because you would have already. So why all the secrecy?" Zota asks.

"Who I am isn't important. It's safer for both of us right now. If you could remember, you'd know why.

Zota walks to the other side of the bar opposite the kitchen as Ryles pulls a plate of red speckled scrambled eggs, hash browns, and sausage out of the microwave. "Diced tomatoes, no onions, right?" Zota asks.

"Right." Ryles grins, and then pulls one of her throwing knives out of the cutting board on the countertop. She shovels some eggs with the spine of the blade, and then after balancing carefully, rolls the eggs in her mouth.

"I know that, but I don't know your name," Zota says. "But there's more than just business between us. I can't feel it."

Ryles laughs hard and long. She pulls a beer out of the fridge, and passes a second to Zota. He hesitates to take it until Ryles smiles and waves the bottle under his nose. "You can feel it? Feel what? Sounds like your little head talking smack."

Zota looks down; and hunches his shoulders. "A connection. Something more."

"You wish," Ryles says. "Plus, you don't really like me much, remember? Oh yeah, that's right. You don't remember."

Zota looks up. "I had a dream last night."

"Was it a wet one?" Ryles giggles. From under the table Zota pulls out Ryles' auto-pistol and points it at her chest. Ryles' face turns stone cold.

"You wanna put that down, before you hurt yourself," Ryles growls.

"Now I got your attention?" Zota says.

"Undivided."

"I dreamt you and I were in a house, in New Mass. We were living together, and there was another woman, important looking, who didn't like the idea." Zota held the auto-pistol and remained silent.

"Put that down...let's talk," Ryles says.

"We got into a car." Zota narrowed his eyes. "A red sports car. The two of us. The same car that was spinning." Zota winced in pain, and put a palm to his temple, unconsciously lowering the auto-pistol.

"You're confused and stressed out. You haven't been laid in over three months, at least. I would be stressed out too. Now put the gun down," Ryles says.

Zota raises the auto-pistol sharply and Ryles recoils with her hands now raised. "I remember watching you step into the car. I saw a tattoo on your lower back," Zota says

"Ooooh, I get it. You think I'm a clone?" Ryles shakes her head. "Maybe I should have left you for the body bandits."

"You've already lied about being my sister. Maybe you're lying about being my business partner. Maybe you're just some crazy *chica* looking for a man?"

"Don't flatter yourself. And I'm not your *chica*." Ryles says. "I got the contract with your signature on it."

"That doesn't mean a damn thing, since I still don't know who I am," Zota says. "I got a better idea. Turn around and lift up your top."

"Excuse me?"

Zota jerks off a round into the ceiling to the right of Ryles, who snapped her head to the opposite side. Zota flinches and slowly regains his focus on Ryles.

"Fine." Ryles turns around slowly, and then lifts her tank top to reveal a scar in the shape of a scorpion, on her left shoulder blade.

Zota lowers the auto-pistol. "Sorry, I had to be sure."

Ryles storms from the kitchen into the living room, grabs the auto-pistol, and slaps Zota, hard. "That's for being the ass you always were." After tucking the auto-pistol back in her hip holster, she stomps back to her breakfast place at the bar. After one bite of the hash browns, she grimaces. "Yeech. Cold." Ryles places the plate back in the microwave. "Two minutes, start," Ryles commands.

Zota rubs the side of his face and turns to Ryles. "I thought you were going to kill me...once you got what you wanted."

"You're worth more to me alive, right now," Ryles says. "But that might change if you ever pull a gun on me again."

The microwave dings at the same time the front door chimes. Ryles and Zota glance at each other. Ryles pulls her plate out of the microwave. The door chimes again.

"Oh yeah. Some guy, John, called," Zota says. "He said he was coming over, and wanted to know if you'd be home." The door chimes again. Ryles' face turns ashen. She comes up to Zota until they are eye to eye.

"Who did John ask for when he called?" Ryles asks.

"Huh?"

"Who did he ask for?"

"Rals, Rails, or something," Zota says.

An older male voice booms through the door. "Hey! It's John! You in there?"

Ryles put her finger over her lips, and passed Zota her auto-pistol. "Grab the duffel bag in the room. Head out the back."

"The back? What back?" Zota asks.

Ryles points to the terrace. "There's a temp-car on Fifth and Bay State. Meet me in the back of East Ispari Hospital in an hour."

"What's going on?" Zota asks.

"Go!"

As Zota runs to the bedroom, Ryles grabs the rest of her throwing knives from the table. She then re-wraps the towel around her hair.

"I'm coming!" Ryles says. She strolls to the door.

Meanwhile, Zota bounds out through the terrace with the bag.

The door gives way, inching open to the left as Ryles approaches. Two massive hands slowly force the door further open. Ryles wraps her fingers around one of the blade handles.

Once the door is completely open, John, Director of Protocol, and one of the Triad heavies all stand in the doorway. Dried and fresh blood, and bruises, plaster John's head, nose, and mouth. The heavy holds him upright. Director of Protocol smiles. "It appears we have a mutual acquaintance."

Elisa steps into Zota's office to grab some digital photos and a recording, in addition to their wedding license. She trips and falls into a pile of clothes.

Aalin hears Elisa scream, and runs upstairs.

Elisa spies an object beneath the bookshelf as she attempts to get up. She focuses with one eye to see a media card. When Elisa hears footfalls in the hallway, she scurries for the card, and slips it into the cybernetic reader embedded in her wrist.

Aalin walks into the room. "Are you all right?"

Elisa slowly rises. "Just a bit of a tumble. Nothing to bother about."

"Are you sure?" Aalin asks. "Let me take you to the hospital."

"No, I'm fine," Elisa says.

"Okay. We should get to Ispari then," Aalin says. "We don't want to risk your husband remembering things we don't want him to." Aalin cradles Elisa in his arms and they both embrace. We see Elisa stare into space while Aalin's voice fades into the background. Elisa's eyes begin to glaze over with bits of code swirling across. Suddenly, her eyes turn from brown to crimson.

Zota scurries down the hill behind the house and through

the parking lot, and into the recreation area. Through a side route, he runs into a cross street. Zota looks behind and around him frantically. He sees no one, and then strolls briskly down the street, further away from the apartment. Ahead, Zota sees an intersection with a main street.

At the intersection of Second Street and Bay State Avenue, a bus whisks by Zota. Zota looks in both directions, and sees a bus point on the left and runs to it. On the area map a red circle flashes around the text, "YOU ARE HERE". Zota taps and holds the map's zoom control, until he can orient himself to his surroundings on the map.

The image of a handsome, thin faced man with short hair overlays on the map. "*Good afternoon? How may I be of service?*"

Zota turns his attention to the virtual assistant. "I need to get to Fifth and Bay State, fast!" The map begins reorienting itself, and plots the optimum path based on Zota's request.

"*Go one half-mile, east, by taxi...*"

"No!"

The virtual assistant receded into the screen. "*I'm sorry, but the next bus won't arrive for another thirty-seven minutes.*"

"I'll walk," Zota says.

"*Judging by your perspiration, your load, and labored breath, I would recommend resting for five minutes before proceeding.*"

"Thanks, I'll walk slowly."

Director of Protocol hovers over to Ryles, who is being suspended a couple of feet in the air by one of his heavies.

John lays crumpled on the living room couch next to them, in a fetal position, barely conscious.

"I suppose I wasn't very clear that I expected you not to disappear for three months. It's very uncharacteristic of you. Which is why you are still alive," Director of Protocol says. He nods to his heavy, who drops Ryles to the ground. After coughing for a bit, Ryles turns on to her back slowly, wincing in pain. "We can do this all day," Director of Protocol says.

"Why..why don't you just...put a bullet in my head? Spare me...the lecture?" Ryles asks.

Director of Protocol whisks his finger up, and the heavy lifts Ryles off the ground again. "Well, I do have approval from the Triad due to your breach of contract." Director of Protocol fans his hand as he swivels his hover-chair around. "We have searched this place from end to end, and have found no sign of the ware. I take no pleasure in wasting life, especially since you have done good work for us in the past."

"Don't get sentimental on me. You're not the type," Ryles says.

"The Triad has the right to...terminate your employment, and has shown restraint in exercising it. So why are you so eager to die," Director of Protocol asks.

Ryles grins "Maybe I'm tired of it all."

Director of Protocol nods, and his heavy drops Ryles again. Ryles moans in pain. The Director hovers to the entrance to the terrace. "Maybe you found a better offer? Maybe you thought, if I get burned, let me burn everyone else?"

"Maybe...you should...lay off the drugs," Ryles says.

"You ought to know," Director of Protocol hisses. He hovers back to the heavy. "Throw him off the terrace, and put her into the car."

Elisa stares out across the bridge connecting New Mass to Ispari and then her view drifts to the dunes beyonds. The sky is clear and the temperature is still high enough that the air conditioning is on high. "It's a shame what the civil war did to this valley," Aalin says. "Thank God we won."

"Did we?" Elisa rubs her hands on her belly. Suddenly Elisa hears a voice. She spins her head to Aalin. "What was that?"

"What was what?" Aalin replies.

"Nothing." Elisa composes herself.

"Well...you have to admit, It was easy for the *daiswrights* and *excretas* of New Mass to put you in office after that. With their crossing to Ispari foiled, they had nothing. No food, no water. Not a hole to bury themselves in. What choice did they have but to accept the terms of the new constitution, and integrate into the caste system for their welfare chips?"

"He seems resentful. Don't you think." Elisa hears in her head.

"Jealous?" Elisa responds.

"Jealous, of what?" Aalin asks.

"That you chose Zota over him."

"Well, I married a *daiswright* instead of a *plutocrat*," Elisa says.

Aalin walks back towards Elisa. "You needed a pretty face for the photo ops during your campaign. I get it. You needed someone that could help pull the *daiswrights* to your side, and see you as the best of the worst. Your mistake was keeping him around too long. Long enough to become a liability. My mistake was not taking care of the liability when your poll numbers first began to slide."

Their sport luxury vehicle reaches the Ispari end of the bridge. Guards at Ispari border gate control scan their passports. The guard reviews the analysis on Elisa's passport, and then does a double-take when he reads the caste details. "My apologies ma'am." He quickly waves at the gate sensor to allow them through. "It's procedure."

"Well you wouldn't want to make it appear you're too eager for a seat at the table of power, now would you?" Elisa asks Aalin.

"He can't be trusted to be satisfied with whatever he gets." The voice in her head whispers.

"I've paid my dues, Elisa. I'm not going to let a ghost from your past take what's rightfully mine," Zota says.

"He means rightfully ours, doesn't he."

Elisa turns away back to the glass, looking back out the window as the vehicle speeds into Ispari. Her gaze is haunting and vacant.

Zota arrives at the corner of Normandy Avenue and Fifth Street. He scans his surroundings after wiping the sweat off his brow. His chest heaves and falls, and his lungs burn. "Man, I'm out of shape." Zota begins to dig into the bag while it's still slung on his shoulder. He drops to one knee, placing the bag on the ground once it proves too cumbersome to attempt a one-handed search. Zota opens the bag up just wide enough to fit his hands. Soon, Zota hears two sets of footfalls approaching. The footfalls slow down and Zota pretends to feel around the bag. When the footfalls stop, Zota looks up. Two large teenage boys are about four meters in front of him.

"You need help," a teenager sporting a mohawk says.

"No thanks. I'm just looking for my water bottle," Zota replies.

"That wasn't a question man," the other teenager with tattoos on his bald skull says. He laughs.

Zota's hand brushes over Ryles' auto-pistol. He stops cold.

Seconds later Guard Practice, swooshes by in a hover cruiser. She sees two teenagers towering over a man stooped over, and pulls over.

"Yo! *guardie,*" the mohawk teenager says.

"You're lucky day pops," the tatooed tenageer says, "let's hover."

Zota hears their footfall move away from him. He exhales and releases his grip on the auto-pistol. He hears more steps from the opposite direction.

"Are you okay sir?" Guard Practice asks.

"Yeah." Zota rises up and turns around. When he sees Practice he smiles nervously. "I'm looking for a rent-a-hover station at Normandy and Fifth. Those kids weren't much help though."

"Actually, if you follow those kids through the mall parking lot, you can't miss them. Look for the yellow signs in the first row," Practice says.

"Thanks," Zota replies.

Back in the vehicle the computer broadcasts and calls to Practice. She waves off to Zota and dashes back to the hover-cruiser.

Patel and Practice arrive at the address next to Ryles' apartment. An older woman rushes out to their hover cruiser waving frantically.

Their hover-cruiser hisses to a stop a meter in front of the woman's dress like someone interrupted her shower. Patel and Practice step down from the cruiser.

"Oh my God. It was awful, just awful. They just threw him out like a bag of trash," she says.

"Calm down, ma'am…" Patel says.

The woman waddles to the side of the house she came out from. "This way!" She leads Patel and Practice beside her house, and then to the back. Splayed out over inflatable pool furniture, is John, bloody and bruised.

Patel pulls his auto-pistol and begins scanning the area. Practice sprays on some insta-skin, waits a few seconds, and then checks John's pulse. "He's dead." Practice tap her earpiece, "Med-unit to my twenty, subject dead at scene." The older woman gasps at the body, and then turns away. Practice comes beside her. "Can you identify who did the throwing?"

"Oh yes. He was a big fella. Like that wrestler on *Friday Night Fights*," she says.

"Was there anyone else involved?" Practice asks.

"Yes. A few minutes after the man threw the guy over, a fat man in a hover chair came out. After him, the same big fella. The big fella, put a woman in the trunk of his car."

"Did the woman look like this?" Patel shows the older woman an image of Ryles on his PDA. The older woman squints, and then turns her head from one side to the other.

"Well, it could be her, but I dunno. I mean they all kinda built the same you know," the older woman says.

"Yes. We know," Practice says. "What type of vehicle was it? What color?"

"It was one of those temp cars, you know? Rent by the

hour… A red one I think. Yes, it was red," the older woman says.

"How do you know it was a temp car?" Patel asks.

"It had the logo on the back," the older woman says. "I passed when I was walking Reginald.." Patel and Practice were about to respond. "..my dog. It was too new and cheap, to belong to anyone on this block. We like the old stuff. You know, cars that last at least five years."

A temp car with the Director of Protocol in the back and his heavy driving hum down the avenue. He hears faint banging beyond the rear cabin he's seated in.

"I guess you didn't drop her hard enough," Director of Protocol says.

Zota breezes through city traffic. He peeks at the GPS clock on the heads-up-display. "Damn."

Morefishco reclines at his desk. His wireless earpiece flashes blue, as he puts notes to net-paper. "What about John Doe?"

On a split display atop Morefishco's desk, Patel appears. *"Ah, he got away from us."*

"Got away?" Morefishco. "How does a man who doesn't even know his own name, in a state he doesn't live in, get away from a state guard?"

"John Doe and Misses Brown were gone when we got to

her residence. A neighbor says some men put Misses Brown in the booth of a temp car. We have another John Doe; dead at the scene," Patel says.

"Great!" Morefishco says. "Any more good news?"

"I've got a trace on our first John Doe," Patel says. *"He is travelling down Main Street. His destination is...East Ispari Hospital."*

A virtual desk guard pops his head into Morefishco's office. Morefishco waves him forward. Behind the virtual desk guard, Morefishco can see Elisa and Aalin. "Have them wait a moment." Morefishco tells the virtual desk guard.

"Please be mindful of the two minute warning," the virtual desk guard says.

"Yes, I won't keep them waiting for more than two minutes. I know the regulation," Morefishco says. Morefishco waits until the virtual desk guard has retreated, before turning his attention back to Patel. "Bring him in."

"On what basis?" Patel asks.

"Driving without a license for starters," Morefishco says, and then taps the screen to end the call. Morefishco waves Elisa and Aalin into his office. He studies them with his glance as they sit down in suits that look like they would cost him a week's salary.

"Thank you for coming Representative Citysun. Can I get you some coffee, water..." Morefishco gestures over to his well appointed minibar, including juices and carbonated soft drinks.

"Zota Citysun is my husband," Elisa says in an even tone. "Where is he?"

Morefishco waits a moment, gazes at Aalin, and then returns his gaze to Elisa.

"This is my protective detail," Elisa says.

"Well, before I can answer your question, I'll need to verify you are who you say you are," Morefishco says.

"Really? You don't know who I am?" Elisa slides forward, leaning towards Morefishco. "Do I need to call your superiors?"

"Don't take it personally. After the week I've had, I'd ask Jesus Christ for I-D, and he can walk on water." Morefishco slides a print scanner in front of Elisa.

Elisa straightens up, and places her right hand on the scanner.

"I guess you don't get net news here in Ispari?" Aalin says.

Morefishco swivels to Aalin. "We do, but I figured why let a few million dollars worth of technology collect dust. On a net-paper display, Elisa's identification and credentials are verified. Her dossier includes the name and picture of her husband.

"Zota...Citysun. I didn't think he was a John", Morefishco says.

"Now that we've established my identity, I would like to see my husband, now," Elisa says.

Morefishco glances at his PDA momentarily as if to will it to chime with a news flash of Zota's capture.

"Well, he's going to be under observation for at least another hour…" Morefishco says.

"Observation?" Elisa asks.

Morefishco holds up his bands. "Just as a precaution, so the department isn't liable for anything that happens to Zota, after we release him into your custody."

"You're stalling," Aalin says.

"Am I?" Morefishco says.

"Yes. What I want to know is why," Aalin says.

"Departmental protocol." Morefishco shrugs. "I'm just a cog in the system. I know *you* understand."

"That's bull!" Aalin says.

"You think I want to keep a three-month-old John Doe case open? Believe me, It'll be good riddance!" Morefishco turns to Elisa. "No offence."

"None taken," Elisa responds.

"You sure I can't get you both a cup of coffee?" Morefishco asks, and gestures again to the mini-bar. Elisa shakes her head. "You're pretty lucky you know? No sign of your husband in three months, and one sunny morning, blam. It must have been tough. I figured you'd be luckier and find him sooner. I'm sure you spent the last three months looking under every rock for him."

Elisa's eyes go vacant and then flicker red. Morefishco doesn't notice.

"Relax! He doesn't suspect a thing. He's just a graying civil servant, grasping at straws," the voice hisses inside Elisa's head.

"Guard Morefishco, I have been more than patient under the circumstances. Now, I would like to see my husband, please," Elisa says.

Morefishco looks to Elisa and then to Aalin and back. "I'll check with my men at the hospital." Morefishco picks up his PDA and pings Patel.

A red temp car pulls into the parking lot of East Ispari Hospital. Once parked, one of Director of Protocol's heavies pops the trunk remotely. He casually strolls to the rear of the temp car, smiles and carefully lifts Ryles out of the trunk, and places her on her feet. Ryles knees buckle, and the heavy catches her and stands her upright. After taking a moment to straighten her up, the heavy passes Ryles her PDA.

Ryles approaches the entrance of the emergency room, her face weathered. She swipes an entry on her PDA and initiates a call.

Patel watches Zota stride into the parking lot of East Ispari Hospital. He glances to his left, and right, and then over his shoulder, pulling the duffel bag he's carrying closer to his body. "I'm looking at him right now chief. Misses Brown also just showed up to, with company. Yes, we are going to need back-up. One is a cyborg."

Patel ends the call, and then sighs. Practice looks at Patel with anticipation. "What did the chief say?"

"The John Doe is Zota Citysun, some New Mass politician's husband. He wants us to protect him at all costs," Patel says.

"What?" Practice asks.

"The chief wants us to bring Citysun to HQ once we get the *all clear*," Patel says. "That's code for: things are about to get very messy, so watch your ass until backup arrives."

"It doesn't sound the same when you say it," Patience says.

Zota sees Ryles stumbling towards him. Her eyes are swollen, and there are cuts across her face. Blood speckles her tank top.

"You look like crap," Zota says.

"Thank you for noticing," Ryles says. "The battered look is making a comeback."

"How'd you get away?" Zota asked.

Ryles tries to grin, and grimaces. Zota fumbles inside the bag until his fingers touch Ryles' auto-pistol. He scans around the parking lot quickly.

"Don't!" Ryles yells.

Zota raises an eyebrow at Ryles and then takes a step

back.

"Why don't you bring the bag to me?" Director of Protocol hovers up from behind Ryles.

Zota spins to make a break for it, only to be greeted by the fist of the Director's heavies. Zota drops into a clump on the ground of the parking lot, after getting his head smacked back. Ryles shakes her head, and walks up to Zota on the ground. "He does you no good brain dead." Ryles taps her forehead with her finger. "Unless you don't want the ware anymore."

"Say you're sorry," Director of Protocol says to his heavy.

"I am sorry," the heavy replies. The heavy goes through Zota's clothing, and finds nothing. The heavy begins to poke into the bag when a voice booms around him.

"Ispari State Guard!" Morefishco yells. "Get face down on the ground with your hands out where I can see 'em.

The heavy glances at Director of Protocol, while still in a prone position with a hand in the bag. Ryles slowly drops to her knees, then to the ground.

Director of Protocol makes eye contact with the heavy and nods. The heavy flexes his muscles and sprints with the bag in one arm. Tear gas grenades fly between the heavy and Director of Protocol. Ryles crawls with her breath held groping ahead. The heavy's feet ignite and a rocket blast lifts him off and towards Director of Protocol. Director of Protocol taps a button on his wrist, and smoke and fireworks stream out of his hover-chair. A swarm of Ispari State Guards open fire with heavy explosive squash head rounds, as the heavy grabs Director of Protocol and blasts off into the evening sky.

As the smoke clears, Zota begins to regain consciousness. He strains to get his bearings and sees a dozen armor units around him. He drops his head in resignation.

"Let me guess," Morefishco's voice crackles through the armor unit's comm system. "That was your crazy uncle, and second cousin, right?" Morefishco waves to Practice and Patel, who both help Zota up. Morefishco leads them towards the collection of cruisers outside the perimeter of the parking lot.

"Should we cuff him?" Practice buzzes through the comm system of her armored unit. Patel stifles a laugh which comes out of his armored unit's comm system as a static. Morefishco grins.

"I don't know. *Zota*? Should we cuff you?" Morefishco asks. Zota looks up to Morefishco, who sees recognition in his eyes. "Yes, that's your real name."

"I haven't done anything wrong, have I?" Zota says. "Besides, how do you know that's my real name."

"You don't have to take my word for it," Morefishco says. "I'm just trying to get rid of you. Maybe it'll stick this time." Morefishco leads them to a cruiser with Elisa and Aalin in the back seat. Morefishco raps lightly on the driver's side of the roof. The guard gets out, and then opens the rear door. Elisa slides out, her exposed, long legs first. Zota sees this and narrows his eyes. When Zota's eyes meet Elisa, she gasps.

Elisa runs to Zota and throws her arms around him. She holds him tight. After what seems like an eternity, she breaks her embrace.

"Elisa? You're Elisa," Zota says.

"Yes. I'm…," Elisa starts, but Morefishco puts up a hand at Elisa interrupting her.

"Zota? Who is she?" Morefishco asks.

"She's…she's…my wife," Zota says.

"I love happy endings, don't you?" Morefishco says with a deadpan expression.

As Elisa embraces Zota again, his and Aalin's eyes meet.

"Who's that?" Zota asks Elisa.

Elisa turns around to follow Zota's gaze. "A friend. He helped me find you."

Morefishco glances at Aalin and then turns to Patel and Practice. "Please give Congresswoman Citysun and her…delegation…an escort to the DMZ."

The stars shine bright and the moon is full. Practice and Patel's armored personnel carrier leads Elisa's vehicle towards the DMZ. Inside Elisa's vehicle Aalin drives while Elisa and Zota hold each other close in the back.

"Guard Morefishco told me you lost your memory," Elisa said. "I didn't believe it."

Zota's eyes drift from Elisa's to Aalin staring back through the rear-view camera display. "I don't remember him," Zota says.

"Aalin is my envoy. You don't remember do you?" Elisa

says. "He was over the house a few times during last summer."

Aalin grins but Zota doesn't see him. The convoy reaches the DMZ tower gate. Aalin passes the checkpoint gate guard his passport. The guard reviews it, looks at Aalin, and gives him his passport.

Practice and Patel watch as the massive gates slide apart and Elisa's vehicle drives through. Practice and Patel watch the DMZ gates shut with a clang behind Elisa's vehicle.

"So is that what they're calling gigolos these days?" Zota says.

Elisa's mask of a smile disappears. "How dare you lecture me on fidelity. If you hadn't left with that whore we wouldn't be in this situation." Elisa slides away from Zota towards her door. "Now we can drop this farce." Her chest heaves and drops. "You could have told me about your contact with the Triad."

"I may be just a *daiswright*, but even I know that the government can't handle the responsibility for that type of ware," Zota says.

"But, I was your wife! I had a right to know!" Elisa says.

"And to get paid," Zota says.

"It was never about the money," Elisa says.

"It is now," Aalin says. He taps the auto-drive button on the vehicle controller. He then turns an auto-pistol on Zota.

"Bad news," Zota says. "I don't have the ware. So, you

have nothing."

"I know," Elisa says. Elisa's eyes flash red, and Zota looks at her closely. "However, I'll have to thank her for leading me to such a payday, with your ware." Elisa brings up her wrist and points to the media slot.

"So why bother to look for me?" Zota asks.

Silence fills the vehicle as Zota looks at Aalin and Elisa's expressions.

"You thought I was dead, but when Morefishco found me it ruined your happily-ever-after," Zota says.

A female silhouette stands in the middle of the bridge between Ispari and New Mass. Coming towards her are the lights of a vehicle.

In her gloved left hand is a device with a flashing red light. In her right hand is a submachine gun. A gloved thumb squeezes the device.

Zota looks to Elisa, who turns to look out the window, staring at nothing in particular.

"Time to put the X in ex-husband," Aalin says. Aalin grins as he lines up the pistol to Zota's head.

Zota looks to Elisa. "For what it's worth, I'm sorry. For everything."

Explosions strike in front of Elisa's vehicle. The vehicle

shudders from the impact and then lurches to the left, then to the right. Aalin frantically attempts to stabilize the vehicle.

"Aalin!" Elisa screams.

The vehicle collides nose first into the guard barrier. Elisa and Zota are tossed to the floor of the vehicle. The vehicle grinds to a halt in front of the woman with the submachine gun at her side. Before Aalin can get his bearings, she races to the driver's side and bashes the glass in. "Out! Nice and cool," Ryles says with the barrel pointed at Aalin's head. She hears movement in the rear of the vehicle. "You too princess!"

"If it's money…" Aalin begins. He looks up but can't only hear a voice in the darkness. He opens the door and steps out slowly.

"Shut up!" Ryles slams Aalin in the face with the butt of the submachine gun, knocking him down to his knees. Elisa steps out carefully from the rear of the vehicle, followed by Zota.

"Do you know who I am?" Elisa asks.

"Yes, I do. And by this time tomorrow, so well everyone on the planet," Ryles says. She looks at Zota. "Tie them up." Ryles tosses Zota a pair of strip binders. Zota catches them both and begins to cuff Aalin and Elisa to the vehicle.

"What are you doing?" Elisa says.

"You tried to kill me." Zota says. "I guess I was some kind of bastard. Ryles levels the submachine gun at Elisa on cue.

"You weren't always like that," Elisa says.

"You're either crazy or stupid." Aalin feels the fresh blood on the side of his face as he steadies himself onto his knees. "You're not really going to kill a *dulcet*, a congresswoman?"

Ryles hits Aalin again with the submachine gun, knocking him unconscious. She turns her attention back on Elisa. Elisa's eyes begin to dart about, and tear up. "I'm pregnant!" Elisa blurts out.

"What?" Zota says.

"That's a good one," Ryles says.

"It's yours," Elisa says to Zota.

"She's playing you, again," Ryles says.

"You'd choose your whore over your own child," Elisa asks Zota.

"I don't believe you," Zota says. "Give me the ware, and I'll disappear, like you wanted me to in the first place. We'll call it even."

"Scan me," Elisa says, looking at Ryles.

Ryles flips on her shades, which shows a thermographic image of Elisa. The view zooms in lower, and a secondary body, pulses fasts, and is white in color.

"She's definitely knocked up," Ryles says.

"But is it mine?" Zota asks.

"I'm not a whore," Elisa says.

"I'm not a killer," Zota says, "but here we are."

Blue and red lights flash against Elisa's vehicle. Ryles turns around in the opposite direction. "You'd better wrap this up. We've got company." Zota sees a barrage of blue and red flickering in the distance.

"Let me keep the ware, and I'll tell you whose it is," Elisa says. "If you don't believe me."

Zota moves in closer, and stares into Elisa's eyes. They are red and vacant. "I don't know how, but we may have a problem," Zota says to Ryles. "The ware somehow infected her."

"So we take her with us, until you can sort it out, but we gotta go..now!" Ryles says.

"Are you kidding? We'll have the whole of New Mass looking for us, not to mention Morefishco," Zota said.

"You got a better idea?" Ryles asks.

"I've got a much better idea," Zota says. "D-M, shutdown code one-eight-november." Ryles eyes immediately rollback white in her head and she collapses into Zota's arms. Zota lays Elisa gently on the ground. He then grabs her left wrist with the embedded media interface and twists it until it pops off.

"Crap!" Ryles said. "You did it."

"Now let's go get paid," Zota says, placing Elisa's detached wrist in his pocket.

"Thirty percent," Ryles says.

"I thought it was twenty," Zota says.

"Ryles bounds over the side of the bridge. Zota follows Ryles over, and down into the night.

THE END